You Belong to Me

Mamoru Suzuki

I love you so much.

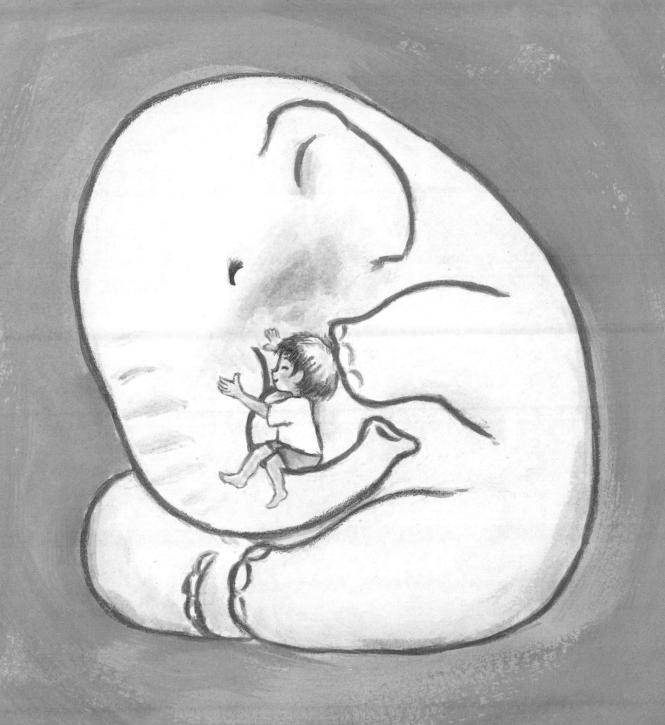

You are my favorite person
in the whole world.

I could spend all day
with you.

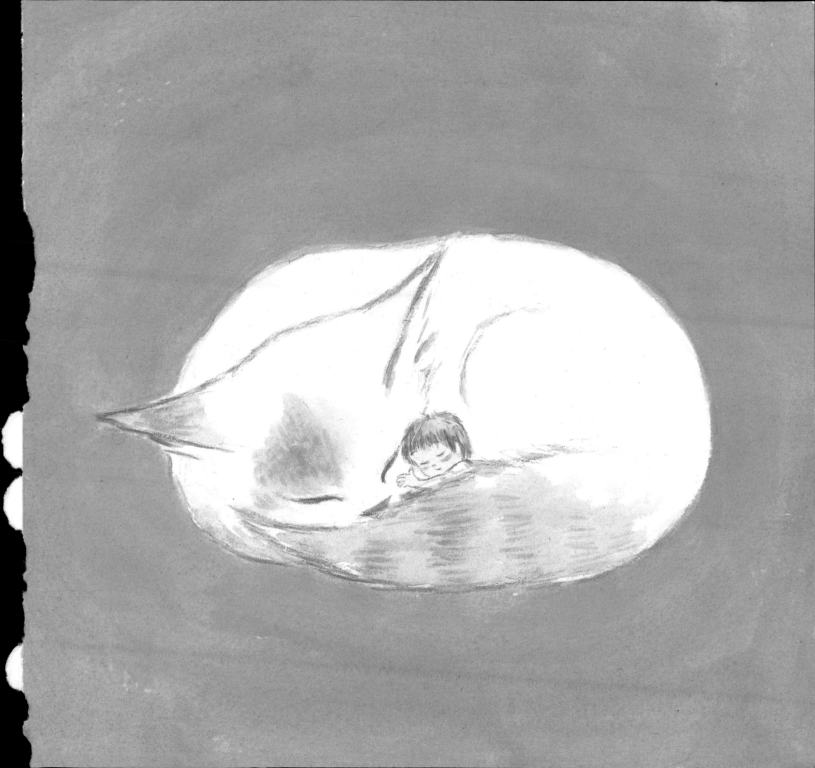

I'll always protect you.

I'll take you anywhere
you want to go.

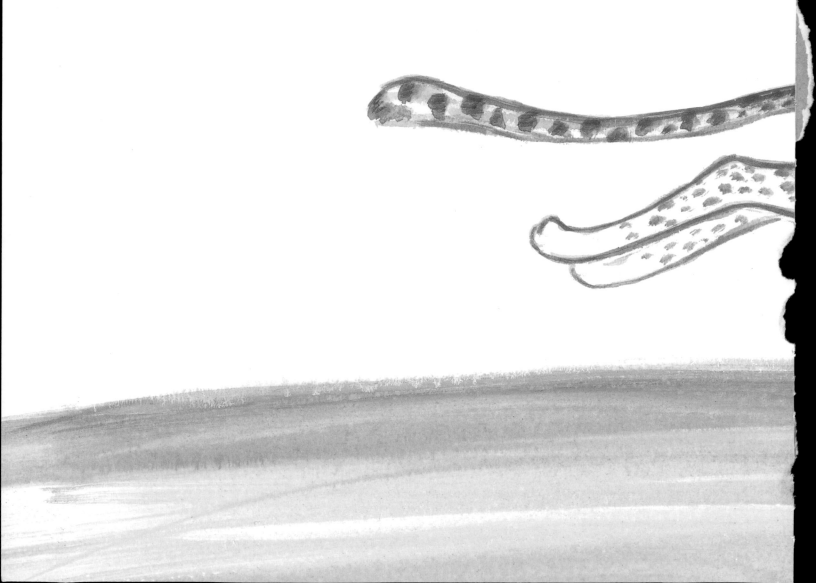

Come to me whenever
you are lonely.

Come to me whenever
you can't sleep.

I'll hug you when you are sad.

I'll lick your tears
when you cry.

We'll stroke your hair
when you are tired.

We'll be there
whenever you need us . . .

Wherever you need us . . .

However you need us.

We all love you.

But I love you most of all,
because . . .

you belong to me.

I am so happy
when we are together.

You Belong to Me

Translation by Mariko Shii Gharbi
English editing by Simone Kaplan

Published in the United States by:
Museyon Inc.
1177 Avenue of the Americas, 5th Floor
New York, NY 10036

Museyon is a registered trademark.
Visit us online at www.museyon.com

Originally published in Japan in 2002 by POPLAR Publishing Co., Ltd.
English translation rights arranged with POPLAR Publishing Co., Ltd.

Printed in China

ISBN 978-1-940842-12-7

1561230